BETTY STOPS THE BULLY

Written by
Lawrence E. Shapiro, Ph.D.
and Illustrated by
Steve Harpster

Author: Lawrence E. Shapiro, Ph.D.
Illustrator: Steve Harpster
Graphic Design by: Chris O'Connor

Summary: This book is intended not only to help the victims
of bullying, but also children who act like bullies as well as
children who are bystanders. Bullying is a serious problem,
but research shows that the more children are aware of the
hurtful effects of bullying, the less it will be tolerated.

ISBN 0-9747789-1-5

Published by:
CTC Publishing
A Division of Courage to Change
10400 Eaton Place, Suite 140
Fairfax, Virginia 22090
703-383-3075
Fax: 703-383-3076
Web Site: www.couragetochange.com

For special discounts on volume orders,
please call 703-383-3075.

To The Boys and Girls Reading This Book,

My name is Dr. Larry Shapiro. Some children call me Dr. Larry.

Even though I'm a doctor, I don't help children with colds or stomach aches or broken bones. I help children understand their feelings and the feelings of other people. I also help children when they are having problems with their friends or with other children at school.

This book is about bullying and teasing. That is a problem for many children. I bet you know someone who has been bullied or teased. You may have been bullied or teased yourself. I can remember being teased when I was a boy because I was chubby. The teasing made me feel very badly, and to this day, I still feel badly when I think about it. Teasing and bullying hurts for a long, long time. I wrote this book to help children like you deal with teasing and bullying. I hope the things you learn will keep bullies and teasers away.

Maybe you have teased or bullied other children yourself. If that is so, I hope this book will help you to stop doing these things. Bullying and teasing is always wrong. It not only makes other children unhappy, it will make you unhappy, too.

Never be afraid to talk to your parents or teachers if someone is bothering you. The more you talk about bullying and teasing, the better things will be.

Your friend,
Dr. Larry

There are many
kinds of bullies.

Some bullies tease
other children.

Some bullies make
fun of other children
and call them
names.

The worst bullies
hurt other children
by hitting them.

All children need to know
that bullying is wrong.

All children need to know
that teasing is wrong.

All children need to know that
making fun of other children is
wrong.

Bullying and teasing hurts children and gives them bad memories for many years.

Look how sad Betty looks!

No one knows why some children are mean to other children.

Maybe they think it will make them popular.

Maybe they are angry and they need some way to let their anger out.

Maybe they are jealous of what other people have.

Being mean to other children makes bullies unhappy, too.

Bullies have fewer and fewer friends as they grow older.

No one knows why some children are teased and bullied more than other children.

Children who are picked on a lot are called "victims."

Bullies often pick on smaller children.

Do you bully and tease other children?

Sometimes children pick on their
brothers or sisters.

Some children watch while their friends are bullied.

These children are called "bystanders."

Have you ever watched while another child was being picked on? Sometimes it is hard to know what to do.

The best thing to do is tell a grown-up right away.

Look in the mirror and what do you see? Do you see a bully or someone who stops bullying and helps other people?

If you tease or bully other children, you need to stop doing this.

Teasing and bullying are always the wrong thing to do.

Bullies often pick
on children who
are alone a lot of
the time.

Bullies often pick on children
who look like they won't do
anything but cry or run away.

Betty got picked on nearly
every day at school, and this
made her feel very bad.

Sometimes children
pick on other children
who look different.

Betty didn't know why other children made fun of her. They just did.

If other children pick on you, there are things you can do about it.

Betty told her teacher that other children were teasing and making fun of her.

A teacher, parent, or counselor might be able to stop bullies. More importantly, they can teach you good ways to handle bullies.

Many children deal with bullying by just keeping away from them.

Betty learned that bullies wouldn't bother her if she always walked with a friend.

She also learned to avoid places where bullies hang out.

If a bully does pick on you, tell him you don't like it.

Just say the same thing over and over again:

"I don't like being picked on. I don't like being picked on. I don't like being picked on."

You can also make sure your body language tells bullies that you are not a victim.

Stand up straight.

Look people straight in the eye.

Keep your hands by your side, not in your pockets.

Humor can help.

Some children use humor to show bullies they are not afraid.

Betty had one joke she felt was very funny.

Do you know why the chicken crossed the road? Why don't you leave me alone and go ask her?

In every school there are some children who pick on other children.

But this happens much less if everyone says:

If you see a child being teased or bullied, see if you can help:

1. Say that bullying is wrong.

2. If you can, ask the child who is being picked on to walk away with you.

3. If you can't think of what to do, get an adult right away.

Do you have an anti-bullying program in your school?

I bet you do.

Betty joined the No More Bullies Club at her school, and she was elected to be the head of the club.

Ask your teacher what your school does to prevent bullying.

Do you talk about bullying and teasing at home?

Sometimes parents don't know if their children are being bullied or teased.

Make sure you always tell your parents if you are being picked on.

Betty asked her parents what they did to keep bullies away when they were children. She learned that her father was teased, just like she was.

Betty reads the No More Bullies Pledge to the kids in her club at the beginning of each meeting.

THE PLEDGE

I promise not to pick on other children.

I promise not to tease other children.

I promise to be considerate of other people's feelings.

I promise to look after other children, particularly if they are smaller or younger.

I promise to tell an adult if I ever see anyone teasing or bullying anyone else.

Here is what Betty learned about bullying.

Bullying is wrong.

Teasing is wrong.

Making fun of other children is wrong.

Bullying and teasing hurts children and gives them bad memories for many years.

If you are picked on by other children, tell an adult.

Keep away from bullies and children who tease you.

Don't stay by yourself. Always walk away or play with another child.

If a bully does pick on you, tell him you don't like it. Just say the same thing over and over again.

Make sure your body language tells bullies that you are not a victim.

Humor can help. Practice some jokes that will make you feel better.

If you see a child being picked on, try to help him or run and tell an adult.

Get involved in the anti-bullying program at your school.

Talk about bullying and teasing with your family.

Take the anti-bullying pledge.

Increasing A Child's Emotional Literacy

Many experts in the fields of mental health and education feel that emotional literacy is as important to a child's school success as traditional academic training. Hundreds of studies have revealed that the people who succeed in life are not always those with good grades and high test scores. In fact, children with good emotional, social, and behavioral skills are more likely to succeed in school and work. They are also more likely to have rewarding friendships and other positive relationships. They are less likely to have mental health problems or to experiment with drugs and alcohol. Children with good emotional skills are even less likely to have physical health problems as they grow older.

The books in the Emotional Literacy Series are intended to introduce children to the many aspects of their emotional education. Each book in the series is designed to explore a particular emotional or social issue, and to get children to start thinking about their behavior. As in any kind of learning, caring and concerned adults can make the difference. Look for opportunities to talk about a child's emotional concerns, and make sure you are a good role model.

Every book in this series teaches children new emotional skills. We hope you will take the time to help children practice these skills and praise them when they use them appropriately.

Remember: **All feelings are okay. It's what you do with them that counts.**

Other Great Books from the Emotional Literacy Series

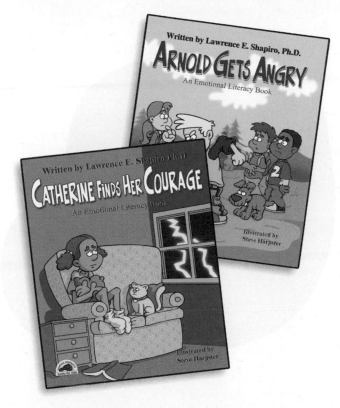

And Coming Soon...

Daniel Defeats Depression
Emma Encounters Envy
Freddy Fights Fat

To place an order or to get a catalog,
please write, call, or visit our web-site.

CTC Publishing
A Division of Courage To Change
10400 Eaton Place, Suite 140
Fairfax, Virginia 22030
1-800-440-4003
www.couragetochange.com